Retirement Writings

An anthology of voices

woven together through

time, memory and imagination.

DIANA SOUTER

Retirement Writings

An anthology of voices
woven together through
time, memory and imagination.

Title: Retirement Writings

First published in 2025 by Kani Consultants, Newcastle, Australia.

A catalogue record for this work is available from the National Library of Australia

The illustration on page 81 was drawn by Leanne Deering.

The cover was designed by Amelia McGarry.

Formatting by Sandra Boyd.

ISBN: 978-0-646-72531-4 Retirement Writings

CONTENTS

PREFACE

This anthology was a little exercise in keeping my brain active after I retired from teaching, studying music and had finished rearing my family. At age 83, after my memoirs honouring my forebears were researched, written and published, and after I retired from conducting the choir my husband and I founded, I looked for a new challenge. I took to compiling short stories for fun and competitions.

Short stories are like tiny nibbles of a new food – bitter, sweet or savoury, fun or serious. The reader may reflect, laugh, cry or just enjoy them. As with many works of fiction, they are not necessarily true, but like all writings, some have truth in experience and background, as do these little stories. Some are prize winners, and some are just fun.

I hope you enjoy spending some time with this collection and they encourage you to write your own. True or false – it's up to you!

A

Dirty

Business

She had been digging in the dirt like her mining forebears before her … deep, deep digging, until one day she unexpectedly hit paydirt! She enjoyed digging into history, a delightful time-consuming pastime she had been looking forward to during this era of the Covid epidemic and enforced isolation. But what she had just found shocked her to the core. Should she continue? Let that hereto unknown scandal see daylight, surface to the top in public view? Could her family's descendants bear the shame?

She couldn't give up now and leave things as before, she had gone too far. But was she brave enough to expose this event in her family's past, mired not in glory but in sorrow and horror? Who else knew of this shameful secret? Certainly, she had no knowledge of it and had never heard it spoken about. Yet here was the evidence, buried in an obscure South Australian newspaper dated 1896! Only a nugget, but a scandalous nugget that rocked her world, the hidden world of her ancestors revealing itself, visible through modern sources of internet searches.

The World Wide Web held secrets, its knowledge contained in unseen ribbons of light hurtling through space. Treasure chests of records – gravestones, newspapers, letters, photos, ancient scandals – lost in the mists of time were waiting to be uncovered. Stories of poverty, wealth and notoriety revealed themselves through her digging and now a mystery – yes, some would say scandal – had surfaced. She had inadvertently hit paydirt! So, she wandered further and further.

The site of her archaeological dig was the internet because that's where the truth about families lay buried. She started searching in South Australia where many of her ancestors lived after migrating from Cornwall in the United Kingdom last century. They came in response to a vigorous recruitment campaign seeking skilled tradespeople and labourers for the early colony. Miners were especially needed after rich deposits of copper and other ores were found in 1841. The Victorian gold rush came in 1851, followed by silver in Broken Hill.

These brave early settlers enduring unimaginable hardships greatly contributed to the wealth of the colony through sheep, wheat, minerals, trades and commerce. Between 1861 and 1901, around 250,000 Cornish miners migrated to the Americas and Australia. There is a saying among them: "A mine is a hole in the ground anywhere in the world with at least one Cornishman at the bottom of it!"

"The Province of South Australia was proclaimed by His Excellency John Hindmarsh at Glenelg on 18th December 1836 who called upon the colonists to be worthy founders of a great and free colony" she read. Well, that's all very well, the researcher thought, but what about me? Where do I fit in?

She was proud to be descended from the pioneer mining families who left their long-buried roots in Cornwall and who came with a hope of putting down new roots in the harsh outback of early South Australia and Broken Hill. These brave settlers in the early days walked a rocky road strewn with hardship. They only endured by possessing an indomitable spirit to survive an unknown future.

She already knew *some* stories …

Her mother was one of eight children brought up in the Great Depression of the 1930s. Her grandmother's husband left her to go walkabout looking for work but never returned, so she had to bring the children up alone. She lived in the same house for 40 years. Her mother had six brothers and a sister, Jean, who in 1932 at the age of 21, was tragically killed in an accident while on the back of a motorbike driven by her then fiancé Jack. Women riding pillion on motorbikes were most unusual in those days, so she must have had spunk! An inquest was held but no charges were laid against the driver of the bike or the car that collided with them.

Musing dreamily, she remembered going as a child in the forties on fun-filled picnics with cousins in Alma Park, sitting under massive old green trees, hooning around on swings and roundabouts, and munching on sandwiches of Devon or Fritz slices with tomato sauce on white bread, no butter. If they were good, they earned a penny ice cream at the still standing and famous Bell's Milk Bar, or a Shelley's soft drink, before they trudged home through the shimmering heat of their summer school holidays. Of course, they were blissfully unaware of skin cancer and the use of sunscreen, the now obligatory outdoor skin protection from melanoma.

Her memories drifted in and out of focus. She remembered how that in the far west, dust storms sometimes raged and ravaged the land. The severity of the storms impacted on the lives of the residents; nothing could prevent sheets of flat iron from being torn from fences and roofs and hurled in life-threatening fashion around the town.

To cool off after the relief of much needed rain, they would play outside with pots and pans or old saucepans filled with the muddy water left in unmade gutters and stormwater drains. There was one scorching hot day at her grandma's when she found herself lying on the green-patterned lino passageway that ran from the front door to the back, trying to catch a breeze.

"One hundred degrees," she screeched in a childish voice, looking at the thermometer and then at the big, brown wall clock, "at only eleven o'clock in the morning!"

"Yes, love, this is Broken Hill, you know," Grandma replied. "Broken Hill summers are fierce furnaces of dry hot air, puffy sandstorms and sweaty bodies."

"When is the iceman coming?" she whimpered.

The air outside shimmers, the ground scorches the feet, plants dry up like the water holes nearby. It would be many years before electric fans or even air conditioners would be installed in ordinary Australian homes.

So, what else did she find digging in the dirt of the past? And why wasn't more known about her great-great-grandparents?

While wandering through the digs, she stumbled upon an astounding gem. A report in the South Australian Registry newspaper of June 1896 read:

The death is reported of the late E M Lowell, of Thebarton at age 74, a colonist of 47 years. Having arrived in South Australia with his parents in 1849 who were engaged to work in the mines, his trade was as a Cabinetmaker. He was a well-known cricketer of 10 years and auditor of two District Councils and well respected in the community. He was the father of 11 children, six still living. As he was found in suspicious circumstances an inquest into his death was held resulting in a verdict of Death by reason of unsound mind.

Wow, this was more than a nugget, this was dynamite! She speculated aloud: could his death have been an accident? Was it the result of a troubled mind brought on by despair or illness? Had he had enough of this hard life? Was there any indication of a cover-up of misappropriation of public funds when he was an auditor? Had he gambled away the family's savings, or could it even have been murder?

Out of three newspapers that reported his death, only one ran the possible suicide story. So how did his family bear this disgrace? Search as we might, the truth will probably never be known, but being the tough pioneers that they were, it appeared that his wife lived for another 21 years. Yes, our researcher thought, 124 years hence, we no longer walk on such a rocky road as it was back then, and we can only admire those forebears who did!

So, dear reader, be brave, get your spade, start digging, you never know what treasures or scandals you may find and maybe the past will trigger your memories, and you will find a nugget – lead, silver or even gold!

The

Innkeeper's

Daughter

The Innkeeper's daughter felt that Broken Hill was inextricably woven into her DNA, her numerous relatives still there after settling the fledgling colony a century before. Excited to be returning there after not having been back since she left as an eight-year-old (except for a holiday when she was twelve), the now grown-up woman was a little apprehensive but also excited to be starting a new job.

Sitting in the steaming train, she glimpsed the emus lolloping alongside the rail on her way to her school at Menindee. It felt like she was coming home. She dreamed about exploring anew, about painting the iconic Sturt's desert pea flowers, and imagined sweating in Silverton where they filmed those iconic Aussie films Wake in Fright and Mad Max. She was proud that the history of Broken Hill was *her* history and that the city contributed so much to the prosperity of a young nation with the silver, lead and zinc mines being at one time the largest and most productive in the world. But who was she and how did she get there?

She was a war baby, born in December 1941 in the Broken Hill District Hospital to Elspeth and Albert in the heat and desert of far western New South Wales to pioneering mining stock, Elspeth and Albert of pioneering mining stock in December 1941 in Broken Hill District Hospital. It was a Monday, under the Zodiac sign of Capricorn and planet Saturn and a fierce westerly furnace of winds. It was also war time, a time of great upheaval in her country and the world.

After the Armistice, the young country, Australia, was an uneasy place, staggering between two world wars and reeling at the shocking loss of manhood. Ongoing rationing ensured people would not put on weight and homemade clothes could be adjusted to last a little longer. Everyone had to eke out a living as best they could.

She was delivered by the first woman doctor Western NSW had ever seen, Franciscka Schlinck, who had come to Broken Hill to find work. This lady was remarkable. Having been born in Germany, Franciscka worked at the Royal Melbourne Hospital, then at Ballarat, where she was sacked because she was a Catholic and she smoked! She joined the staff of Broken Hill District Hospital in 1936, withstanding a hostile reception from the resident male surgeons. This brave doctor was one of the first few women allowed to go underground after she demanded access to treat injured miners.

Her mother Elspeth, the fourth child in a brood of eight, was born on the first of September 1916. Elspeth's first job was at Dryden's Department Store in the main street of Broken Hill on a wage of eleven shillings and six pence (11s 6d) per week. She worked there until she married. As was then the custom, married women did not 'work' outside the home, with very few ever being able to earn and control their own finances, thereby being dependant on their husbands or families. As was the custom in the pre-war days, any dreams women had of further study or a career died when they woke up! Why bother educating them when they were expected to marry, have kids and look after their husbands? It wasn't until after the Second World War that girls were allowed and encouraged to embark on a higher education. With tenacity, courage and hard work they are still doing it – juggling study, a job and a family – but equality of wages is still being fought for.

The Innkeeper's daughter seemed to have inherited this indomitable spirit and never really accepted the fact that girls should be ladylike in their manner. She recalled a time when she was five years old, dressed demurely in her sweet pleated tartan skirt and hand-knitted jumper, starting school lining up for milk – you know, the third of a pint of white, warm stuff – when a rude boy pushed in front of her. Exercising her pioneer spirit, she hit him on the head with her little, red tartan suitcase. After being told off by her teacher, she ran home in disgust. It was her first taste of equality and wow it felt good, even though she was sent home. I won't say that this was the start of her lifelong fight for equal rights for women, but it must have had some influence!

Her father Albert, born 1912 in Adelaide, was an only child. His father Percival was a miner, not very demonstrative or affectionate. Maybe that's where Albert got his reticence. He was a handsome man, tall and thin with a beetling brow and diffident smile, as though he had no right to be happy. A man of that era didn't show emotions, but he was always a kind, if a little aloof, figure that sometimes surprised her, like the time she was boarding the train to travel overseas for the first time at age 21 and he quietly slipped some money into her coat pocket! He also shouted the bar when she graduated from college. His first pub was the Yanco Glen Hotel, set in inhospitable landscape eighteen miles north of Broken Hill. It was a wood and iron building, pretty basic, but with a verandah and a dance hall attached to where, as a baby, she slept amidst the heat, dust and flies.

The Glen itself was one of nature's oases in the far west country of New South Wales. It was first discovered by the explorer Charles Sturt and used by him as a basecamp. The pub catered to station workers, rabbiters, 'roo shooters and travellers to and from the far north of the state, but the main trade was on the weekends with Broken Hill people who would ride or drive out for a drink. On Friday and Saturday nights they would be trading till all hours of the morning. This was in the days of 'the six o'clock swill', not that that mattered much in Broken Hill where you could get a drink till nine or ten o'clock in the closed hotel saloon bar or parlour, often swapping stories with the local constabulary.

The Cobb & Co coaches used to stay at the hotel in the 1800s. The hotel was also a non-official post office. Elspeth was the telephone office keeper with a small switchboard that served several of the stations in the vicinity.

After almost two years at Yanco they sold out, as they had done very well out of it. The building is no longer there and unfortunately the famous original hotel was burnt down some time ago, so there goes another piece of Aussie history!

After Yanco, they packed up the house and her and her Dad, Mum, dog and baby brother set off across the state on untarred roads to the lush green pastures of the South Coast where her Dad had bought the Bodalla Hotel, already a historical landmark. Grandma, her father's mother, who had survived the depression, of course also came with them.

The Innkeeper's daughter's primary school was set in the bush, lunch taken under the huge peppercorn trees. The shield on the school's outside wall proclaimed to all who entered: "To Thyself Be True".

Three years later, the Innkeeper was bitten by the travel bug again, so in 1951 they trundled off in an old rattle trap up to the North Coast to Beechwood near Wauchope, the 'Timber Town'. Their next move was to the London Hotel at Ardlethan in 1954.

She recalled that this year was also the first time a living sovereign had set foot on Australian soil, with Queen Elizabeth and Prince Philip touring all over the country. Seven million Aussies took to the streets to see them, still happy to be part of the British Empire. Yes, there is talk of us becoming a republic, but indecision about how to elect or appoint the president or head of state is not yet agreed. So, following her father's itchy feet, it was back up the North Coast of New South Wales to inn number four, beautiful Sawtell near Coffs Harbour, where she enjoyed the surf and the sun.

Upon returning from an overseas trip, she was astounded to find that her mum and dad, in a strange quirk of fate, had rebought the McConkey's Hotel at Bodalla. The Bennett's and McConkey's having exchanged the hotel twice over the past years. Yes, thought the Innkeeper's daughter, recalling the old school motto "To thine own self be true".

As the train pulled into the railway station, she looked around and sighed. It had taken twenty years and five inns, but yes, the Innkeeper's daughter had finally come home.

The
Wedding
Dress

The day dawned soft and pink, the air already crisp, promising a fine, if cool, day. Fine for that part of Australia usually meant dry, dry and drier, under an endless sky and a bright orange blazing sun. Here in this harsh, red and brown land, the day was sometimes marred by swirling dust storms, the air stirred up with debris from the nearby mines and bullock drays on their way down south to the market town. It left a veil over everything, even over the straggly, grey gumtrees struggling in the bush.

This was Central Australia, spring in the year 1902. For Rosa, it was a year of great promise of marital bliss in her new life as a married woman. Rosa didn't care what the weather was like as she prepared for the most exciting day of her life – her wedding. She felt she was ready, ready to face an unknown future with a man she had been promised to for nine years: nine years of chaste courtship and stolen kisses. Waiting, waiting, through the churning days of unending housework, lost jobs, drought and depression. Her pioneering family had survived life's most challenging times: money worries, sickness and loss. As bleak as this harsh land had been in drought and flood, they were at least looking forward to better times with the opening up of more mines.

The family home of rough bricks and mortar and tin roof already creaking in the heat prepared itself for an influx of guests, relatives and friends, tired and dusty after travelling exhausting miles on horseback and dray. Her mother had spent many hours preparing the house and the wedding feast. Neighbours and fellow church members discussing the merits of one dish over another finally agreed that it should be a traditional one. The kitchen smelled of a celebration of lamb meat pasties, roast vegetables, soda biscuits and fruit cakes cooked in a black iron stove over many hot days. And it was all for her!

Rosa was a petite lady, with a kindly if not classic beauty. All her family were big people, especially her three brothers. She was the fifth child of Charles and Sarah. As the second eldest girl in a large family, she always had plenty to do. Settlers in the early days walked a rocky road strewn with hardship and only endured by possessing an indomitable spirit to survive an unknown future. Having endured the dishwater grey of never-ending housework, she was clinging to the hope of soon turning those grey days to rainbows, and the hope that by marrying a storekeeper, her future would be brighter.

Her husband-to-be was the sixth child of John and Margaret. He was only eighteen when they met while he was working in the local produce store. It was a long courtship for those times – the course of true love never did run smooth – but with determination on the part of both of them they won out in the end.

Her trousseau all packed up in the carved wooden trunk, she lay on the bed surveying the room she shared with her sister Jean one last time. Staring at the flowered wallpaper and the white stucco rose on the ceiling, she wondered what her new life would be like.

"Are you ready yet Rosa?" her mother's voice called out from the kitchen where the wedding feast was being prepared.

"I have been ready for nine long years, Mum" she whispered to herself.

She carefully lifted the dress of virginal white off her bed. Running her hands over it She admired the Irish linen bodice edged with exquisite lace; the tiny, crocheted buttons that had been handmade under a dull lamp light over many months; the long sleeves puffed with layers of lace and finished with satin edging.

The skirt was plain, long and swirling, sewn on a modern marvel, the pedal Singer Sewing machine. This was a moment she had dreamt of for so long. She held her breath and gently slipped it over her head. Her long, dark hair brushed to sheen hung straight down her back.

"I'm ready, Mum," she called. "Come and button me up." At last, it was time! For years, Rosa had dreamed of marriage, not just because she loved Charles, but also because of her Christian faith and because it was normal in her society.

The wedding party emerged from the house. Squinting against the glare of the dazzling sun assaulting their eyes squinting against the glare, they walked the short distance to the church. A faint patina of the past, of mystery and suffering, hung in the air, the Baptist church standing sentinel to the early settler's moral fortitude. Its no-nonsense mudbrick and stone façade and plain, white-washed walls had been softened with enough flowers to grace the altar for a celebration. She was proud that she was the first child baptised in that outback church. Today she would be married in it!

Gliding into the church on her father's arm to the strains of Mendelssohn's *Wedding March* being played on the pedal organ, she smiled with joy, her eyes sparkling like blue sapphires. As her new husband in formal suit and tie gently slipped the wedding ring onto her finger, the choir sang joyously, and her mother breathed a sigh of relief.

Eight children later, through poverty and riches, a dynasty was established. Time passed, mines closed, the great houses were left to ruin, inhabitants scorched by the unrelenting sun and hardship dwindling jobs and moving on. Their sacrifices, their stories, their lives now lost in the mists of time. But what happened to their treasures and to Rosa's wedding dress unseen for more than 120 years? Where did it lie, lost from view, lost from history? It was time to tell its story and how it found its way back home to where it belonged!

As the eldest person in my extended family, the memorabilia of my ancestors spanning over many generations sits in boxes and albums on my downstairs table. Old photographs, letters, programmes, cards and school reports from the long ago past, where-in dwells their history now awaits my selection. Sorting these treasures seems overwhelming and often emotional. "Pick me," they whisper, "for posterity."

Memories, insubstantial yet persistent, redolent of the smells, tastes, emotions felt in their presence persisting long after their demise. I chose some objects, leaving the rejected ones ready to be packed away again, later to be given to other family members. And then suddenly I found it, my grandma's wedding dress, and hidden in its folds a wedding ring all lovingly wrapped in a small silk-lined box. As I slipped her gold ring onto my finger, I vowed to return the dress to its home.

Drama

on the

Indian Pacific

It was a warm September day, and crowds of excited travellers were massing at Sydney's Central Station. The air was abuzz with anticipation as suitcases, backpacks and sunhats jostled for position at the check-in counter. Little did my husband Ron and I know when we boarded the *Indian Pacific* how eventful this journey would become.

It was to be a pilgrimage for my 80th birthday and what an adventure it turned out to be! My plan was to train to Broken Hill, where I was born and my forebears lived 200 years ago, to deliver a very special parcel, and then to head on to Adelaide, change trains and then on to Uluru, that world famous monolith in the centre of Australia.

Arranging our travel itinerary and three weeks of bookings from home on the North Coast of New South Wales to the Northern Territory and beyond was challenging enough, but I also spent many hours setting up appointments in Broken Hill and Adelaide for our once-in-a-lifetime adventure.

After many months of detective work into where I should lay the special parcel to rest, arrangements were made to deliver it personally. At last, the time had come to send it on its long journey home across the state.

I decided it was fitting to travel by rail, so the second part of my modern pilgrimage began on *The Ghan*, the world-famous inland train and the longest, straightest railway line in the world. It ran from Adelaide to Darwin. The arid landscape was still harbouring ghosts of my forebears, pioneers and Afghans who had worked on its construction.

Finally, we were ready to go, and arrangements were made to hand over the precious articles. With a sigh of relief, we found ourselves onboard at last. The train was one kilometre long with 200 passengers there to enjoy the luxurious facilities, bar and restaurant. Our tiny cabin had an ensuite bathroom and a seat that could be made into two bunk beds. Being some years younger than my husband, I offered to do the climb for the top bunk.

Finally, the dress was on its way home. Or was it?

All travel relies on good weather permitting which it did not. With much trepidation We boarded the train in torrential rain. The lead up to the pilgrimage saw unprecedented floods all over the state and transport anywhere was becoming increasing fraught. Flights were being rerouted or cancelled, roads cut, and trains delayed. Floods were forecast for the whole state. We fervently hoped they would not impact on our journey.

The first hiccup was at 11 pm as we were preparing for bed, me in the top bunk in our snug little cabin, when I checked with the guard the time of arrival in Broken Hill.

"Oh no," he said "We are not stopping there now due to floods and track works. There will be no half-day excursions or sightseeing."

My face fell. One of my aims was to personally deliver my Grandma Oliver's wedding dress and a copy of my memoirs to the heritage museum and library. This involved tight timing and legal documents that had to be handed over to a Ms Tracey, the librarian and museum director from the Council, at a small ceremony – covered by the *Barrier Miner* newspaper, of course.

Thanks to the efficiency of mobile phones, frantic texting to Tracey ensued throughout the night. After a sleepless night of not knowing if or how my treasures were going to be delivered, the train pulled into Broken Hill station at 8 am. There was knock at my cabin door and with a smile of self-satisfaction the guard told me we were stopping in Broken Hill, but no one was allowed off.

"But I have to deliver my parcel," I wailed. "I have written my memoirs and have a priceless garment to deliver. Can't I just step off for a moment, please?"

"No, but you can stand on the step, and I will arrange for the train to stop for a short refuel so your contact can grab your parcel." he replied.

Where was my moment of glory, I thought. My smiling image in the newspapers, my relatives welcoming Grandma's dress home? So, imagine my surprise and joy as I stood on tiptoes, hanging out of the window, at spying a lady I presumed to be Ms Tracey running along the platform in the early morning mist, hair flying, arms outstretched to catch the parcel! Waving madly, I screamed "Here, here!"

As she caught up to my carriage the train came to a jolting halt. Embracing through the window opening and crying with relief, I gently passed her the precious parcel. As she hugged it to her and the train pulled out, we waved a tearful farewell.

***

The above is a true story and was reported in the Broken Hill *Barrier Daily* newspaper in August 2022.

> Hundred-year-old dress finds its way back to Broken Hill. In 1908 this wedding dress of fine Irish linen and lace was worn by a young woman as she embarked on her journey into matrimony. And now at last the dress has made the trip home.

Colours

White, everything is white. White skin, white clothes, white shoes, white hair tied back with a white ribbon, white bread sandwiches, white sun in a blazing white sky burning my little white feet on the scorching white sand.

My eight-year-old self-dances down to the picnic beach through the heat of the 1949 Australian summer. The inland lake shimmers, the cool water invites me in to paddle. I meet my two girlfriends, and we giggle behind our hands as we point to another girl – black skin, black hair, black eyes and funny clothes.

Mum says, "Stop staring, they are harmless. They are Afghan people, from afar, brought over with their camels to our inland areas to settle and assist with the construction of roads and railways in the desert many years ago."

Later on, as we motor past an encampment on the outskirts of town, I ask, "Who are those dark people, Mum? Why don't those kids go to school with us?" There is no answer.

The colours change to yellow, brown, black, the sky to brilliant blue. Red is the fury at my 10-year-old self being marched off the school sports field seventy years ago by the headmaster for showing my legs, seething with indignation at not being able to play football with the boys. Today I clap happily as my 14-year-old granddaughter sprints past wearing skimpy, green soccer shorts, whooping with joy and freedom. Soccer! No longer a boys-only game.

At high school, girls with yellow-flecked slanted eyes, lustrous black hair and smooth complexions fed our curiosity and admiration. For their forefathers, yellow gold was the colour of their world, brown the colour of the earth they dug. How I admired them cleverly speaking in a different language. There was only one language in my family and that was proper English. People who weren't born in Australia were deemed "Foreign". But does the need to embrace diversity mean that our modern usage of language is too relaxed, too colourful, too often peppered with the slang and foul swear words that would have my parents washing my mouth out with soap. Black is different. Black skin, black hair, black clothes, the colour of exotic places and races. Travelling overseas, my 21-year-old eyes are opened to a previously unknown world of colourful exotica: faces, languages, customs, dress and food. Oh, the food!

My mature life takes on a more daring hue as I get an education previously thought unnecessary for girls and find myself in a management role in a large city council.

"You will need to move the desks so that Linda, my new secretary, has adequate room to navigate her wheelchair around the desks," I say to the staff at my workplace.

Eyebrows are raised, desks shuffled. Linda is no longer "handicapped" as before, but "mobility challenged" and a worthy participant in our workplace. Workplaces now cater to a variety of ages, colours, sexes, sizes and shapes. It takes time to open people's formerly closed eyes.

Luckily, we no longer live within the strict parameters of a white-world regime, as in George Orwell's novel *1984* with people who were coerced to look and sound the same, but in a joyous freedom of colour painted on a much richer canvas. Living without the parameters of fear of being different, we can be any colour, size and shape we like!

As I think of government, I reminisce at the state of politics. It was exactly thirty years ago that I stood for parliament, representing a very diverse constituency of over sixty races, colours and creeds, and blessed the democracy that allowed them to vote for whomever they liked.

I decide to ignore the discriminatory practise of ageism as I ready myself for an event, grey hair tinted to a fetching shade of auburn, flattering fitted clothes. "Is this lipstick too red?" I ask my new husband.

Too late to fall in love, write a novel? Never! Now my 80-year-old self-celebrates that our society is not an all-white, male or female, young or old, able or disabled world, viewed through the prism of prejudice. and I am glad.

Yes, it is no longer either black or white, the colours of my beloved piano keys. As in the composing of a symphony or a sonata, all the keys, both black and white, high and low, soft and loud on a keyboard are needed to create a tune, a wondrous harmony; the sharps for the ups and flats the downs.

Today as I conduct my choir of oldies, I note the joy on their faces. Blue, brown, grey and black hair, pink cheeks, eyes shining, raising their voices together, singing with joy, songs from different countries and cultures – classical, folk, pop, and jazz.

White is the colour of our shirts, black our pants, as we celebrate our multi-coloured world in concert. We sing together about the rainbow hues colouring our lives. And I give joyful thanks for my long life lived to the fullest with colour, compassion, freedom and yes … plain white!

First

Flight

A deafening, terrifying whine screamed overhead, banking towards the sea, then thinking better of it spun around and made for home. Home was Williamtown airbase, and amid much fanfare the shiny new F-35A Joint Strike Fighter planes had arrived at Port Stephens. They were to be a guardian of our skies, Australia's first line of defence against unwanted intruders. From my balcony, I watched the plane fade into the distance and remembered, as the mind does unbidden, another flying machine at another place and another, more peaceful time – my first overseas flight.

In those long-ago days of my youth in the 1960s, travelling by air was an expensive and glamorous affair. No-one we knew had even been in a plane let alone abroad, and I was the first in the entire extended family to travel around the world in 1964. Was this then the start of my love affair with that opulent airborne taxi?

My first flying adventure occurred in 1962, however, when I went from teaching in the second hottest, furthest west school in New South Wales to the second most easterly school after Norfolk – Lord Howe Island.

This was a two-teacher school, with a headmaster who took the older children and myself who took the little ones. It was set in a World Heritage-listed paradise with magnificent beaches, tangled jungles, pristine clear waters and coral atolls. It had only one drawback – the only way to get there was by ship from Sydney or New Zealand, or by a Sunderland Flying Boat!

The Flying Boat sported four engines, two on each wing a veritable double-decker bus with wings and floaters to land on the water in the lagoon. The upstairs section was decked out as a lounge with cocktails served with panache by a glamorous young hostess. Imagine my excitement at boarding this exotic craft at age twenty. I felt like a celebrity in, wearing my sweet pale blue, short skirt suit and matching earrings and handbag, taking off from Rose Bay in Sydney, having drinkies and flirting with the captain – so romantic and grown up! There were only two of these magnificent craft left by then, many having been lost in Europe during the last war. The Flying Boat serviced the island once or twice a week, the landings carefully timed to coincide with the tides. Sometimes it would breakdown or be late, or miss the tide, disappointing both holiday-makers eager to visit and locals eager for their mail and goods ordered from the mainland. It was also captive to good weather, gliding serenely onto the turquoise waters of the lagoon in-between the coral reef and wild, deep-blue ocean. My young heart would skip a beat each time it landed, as I ran to the jetty to see if my handsome pilot friend would be on it, having met him on my flights home at the end of each school term. The crew – pilot, engineer and hostess – stayed the night and were royally entertained by the local hostelries.

During my tenure of two years, I boarded with Mr and Mrs King, whose ancestors could be traced back to the Mutiny on the Bounty. Philip Gidley King was the third governor of New South Wales from 1800 to 1806. He also set up the penal colony at Norfolk Island. Enroute to Tahiti to gather saplings from the Breadfruit Tree, the crew mutinied, with some survivors jumping ship at Pitcairn. Some of the children at Lord Howe were descended from survivors of that ill-fated trip in 1787.

One of my pupils, Rosanne, looked like a Polynesian princess, with her dark eyes and long, glossy, crinkly black hair. Lord Howe is now known for its relaxing holiday resorts, indoor palm tree industry, and as well as pristine coral diving adventures. As a two-teacher school, the headmaster took classes for those aged from nine to twelve and I took the littlies aged four to eight. Living on a tropical paradise was idyllic, if a little restricted. My free time was filled by playing tennis; listening to records bought from the Readers Digest by post; choosing clothes ordered from David Jones by catalogue; painting local scenes and collecting shells; and then later, planning my first world trip, this sojourn giving me a taste for more adventure.

I learnt to water ski, partied with gusto, and invited famous people visiting on holiday to speak to the school kiddies. Walking carefully to school through jungle, dodging spiders as large as saucers, I marvelled at my good fortune at being chosen for this job. At twenty, I fell in love with a dashing local, who was in the merchant navy. A courtship done in secrecy in a small community of only 300 people was impossible, of course. Gossip was then what today's Facebook is now, and word soon spread. It wasn't all moonlight and roses, however! One fateful night I awoke to the sound of a tin roof slicing through a palm tree, the wind screaming and howling and felling swathes of jungle, and rain lashing the outside of my window. Terrified, I imagined with horror the scene unfolding on the shore below my hill. On this unforgettable night in the violent tropical storm, the tethered flying boat broke its moorings and ended up battered and broken on the local beach.

> "It was carrying a happy band of bowlers enroute from Sydney to Noumea. During the dark early hours came the storm, high winds and heavy seas, the flying boat broke its moorings and flung itself up on to Lagoon Beach. One wing buried itself in the sand and its float smashed. In wind and rain and bitter cold, the intrepid islanders rallying to an emergency as always managed to upright her. With men and tractors pushing and pulling, the one working engine full blast, she slipped back into the water, men sitting on the wings, boats pushing and heaving and smashing on to the coral. Alas one engine was ruined by sand and water; nothing could be done to save her."

What an historical event to witness! My report published in the Sydney Morning Herald, "Death of a Chieftain" (the Flying Boat was named Pacific Chieftain), earned me a reprimand via telegram from Sir Reginald Ansett himself!

Later, a wake was held as they stripped her of oil, engines and furniture. At that time, we were isolated! Luckily, there was one other Beachcomber available to carry on the service for another couple of years, but sadly, the flying boat service doesn't exist anymore. There is an airfield, with small Qantas planes landing three times per week, but where's the romance in that?

Yes, flying then was certainly an adventure and a far cry from today's speedy, luxurious silver torpedos. So, as the shiny new fighter planes roared over my head, flinging themselves into the distance, their roar slowly fading, I pulled myself back to the present and gave thanks for those clever, brave and courageous men or women in their flying machines – in air or over water.

History and progress march on and unfortunately it was in March 2002 that the final Ansett Airlines flight took place. Founded by Sir Reginald in 1935, Ansett had been our biggest domestic airline for seven decades and, having often flown with them, I was sad to see it go.

My final homage was to attend an auction in Sydney of some of the fittings from Ansett's planes – I now savour my boiled eggs from an Ansett egg cup.

Today, there are dozens of local and international airlines flying in Australia and to and from all over the world, but I will never again feel the thrill of that first flying, floating machine and the time that left me bereft at the death of a Chieftain!

Shifting

Sands

Sand. Filling the dry landscape. Hot beneath our feet, gritty in our eyes, filling the dry landscape. The colour of the earth, the colour of the water, the colour of our clothes. Of everything.

The glare was turning the desert landscape to white, the heat turning the river to molten sludge and our skin to paper. Our clothes of loose cotton clung to our legs which were now slimy with sweat and ringed with red heat blotches. So how did my friend and I find ourselves here in this inhospitable place?

On a coming-of-age trip overseas, my 21-year-old eyes were opened to a previously unknown world of colourful exotica: faces, languages, customs, dress and food. But this was something extra special. As a student of ancient history, I was thrilled on our arrival in Cairo to be invited by an archaeology professor to attend a dig in the Valley of the Kings at Saqqara.

It was 1964 and this was a time of momentous world affairs. Dr Martin Luther King was awarded the Nobel Peace Prize, Nelson Mandela was imprisoned for life in South Africa, and King Farouk of Egypt was exiled to Italy. And, of course, the film *Dr Strangelove,* set in the future, was released in the USA. But we were here to explore the past, the long distant past.

Travelling by train from Cairo where we had stayed the night speeding along the bank of the Nile, through desert and tiny villages made of straw and mud, we glimpsed grubby little children playing in the dirt, women carting water on their heads in large jars, and men in long, white robes tending to scrawny cattle.

My friend and I arrived at Saqqara early morning, but the only transport we could afford to take us on our quest to the pyramids was a donkey! Bumping along, frantically clutching the rope reins we whooped with joy – our history lessons had come to life.

The scenery was of intense contrast. The seasonal green belt that extended along the edges of the river soon gave way to desert and decay, all under a blazing blue sky. In front lay a vast valley of undulating sand hills. The only building to be seen was a small pyramid on sentry duty. There were few tourists up so early.

The fabulously unreal landscape shimmered in the heat haze, the sound of our footsteps absorbed by the grand valley as we slowly advanced.

It was here in this ancient Egyptian Kingdom that Pharaoh Tutankhamun held court and commanded life and death over his subjects. I thought of the story and the *'Curse of the Grave Robbers'*. It had been 42 years since Howard Carter was finally granted permission to dig. Forty-two years since he found his way into the Valley of the Kings and into history, unearthing the most extraordinary and valuable archaeology discovery of all time.

Shielding my eyes from the burning glare, I wondered at the sheer scale and awesomeness of these desert treasures, and at the monoliths at Knossos, another amazing site further down along the Nile their stories told on the still legible hieroglyphics on the walls, the massive columns designed and built by brilliant minds unsurpassed in the ancient world. We still marvel today at the amazing engineering feat of these monuments of faith in the afterlife, the various pyramids, and their hidden underground burial spaces. So how did I find myself so enchanted in the home of Ramses, Cleopatra, Nefertiti and Tutankhamun? And more puzzling, how did I find myself lost in that hot sand?

We were here on a grand mission to explore the 'History of Humanity'. With the bravado of the reckless and the curiosity of our ignorant youth, we had been granted special permission to view a newly opened tomb only a week before. This was to be with a guide to show us the way and to keep both us and the contents safe. Of course, it was and is against the law to take anything away and the penalties for grave robbing are harsh.

The hole was deep and revealed a narrow tunnel below. The fetid air, still tangy with death, dust and history. My eyes searching excitedly for light in this scary, dark musty hole, I readied myself to follow my guide into the pitch black, his torch the only light. Squeezing down a narrow opening in the sand my heart was in my mouth with fear and excitement as to what we might find – no artificial lighting or safe stairways or touristy setups were evident here yet. "It was a time of magic on earth," he said. "Of god-like men, colossal battles, giant statues and art and riches beyond belief." I was really glad to have him reassure me as we descended together!

The tomb was very dark with a terrifying air of mystery. Brown painted wooden coffins, pottery and statues filled the airless space, their life stories still reaching to us from the past. Eyes adjusting to the murk, I spied dozens of artefacts all piled on top of each other. Where did such skills and know-how come from thousands of years ago? Some think the answer to that may be further afield than our own little planet. In support of their argument, they note that hieroglyphics have no connection with the Arabic language which was introduced to Egypt when Arabs conquered it.

Intrigued by the mystery but feeling scared to be alone, I wandered off then I was not alone. A shiver snaked up my back and then the light went out! Where was my guide carrying the torch? Feeling as though I was disappearing into blackness, my heart beating frantically, I stopped. "Don't panic," I whispered to myself, "he will find you". But the fear of being buried alive in this dusty airless hole was too terrifying to contemplate.

"Help!" I screamed as I stumbled, bent over in the near darkness of the narrow low tunnels. "Help, help!"

The walls were closing in on me. I was gasping for breath, my heart was racing, my skin exuding the smell of fear. Suddenly, turning a corner, I saw a shadow, a flaming torch attached to the wall giving me just enough light to see. To my joy, my eyes lit upon some hieroglyphics – a painting procession of slave ladies-in-waiting, stiff arms by their sides, pointy faces, straight black hair, bejewelled necks, staring eyes, all facing the same way. Such carvings had long ago lost their colour, but not their message. Were they pointing me to the way out?

Hieroglyphics can now be read by scholars thanks to the 1799 discovery of the Rosetta Stone by French soldiers, the stone enabling the stele to be translated into Greek and Egyptian. And so I did my best to follow those directions, feeling my way along the wall. I thought of Howard Carter finding King Tut's tomb in Luxor's Valley of the Kings and the curse he seemingly brought upon himself with his untimely death due to a lung infection. Are the germs still alive, waiting for their next host? That was the tomb of his dreams, but not of mine. Unlike today, there were no hygienic face masks for protection then.

At last, to my great relief, I saw daylight. As I crawled back through the tunnel out to the entrance, my eyes squinting in the glare, I quietly pocketed a small shard of pottery found on the sand.

Red is the sun as it sinks below the horizon and brown the colour of the earth they dug in, but sand is still the colour of desert dreams. And, oh yes, those curses really do work, because that night I was savagely bitten by bedbugs in our cheap hotel room!

A Home

of

One's Own

The soldier had returned dressed in battle fatigues, tired, worn and dispirited, but determined to succeed in a new life of his own choosing. It was the aftermath of World War Two and change was in the air. In far western New South Wales, the mining boom had fizzled out, the war effort downgraded, and unemployment was rife. It was time for a new life in a new town and a new start for the new wife and new baby. After giving it some thought, Ray hit upon the idea of becoming a publican. Because what do people need to exist? Shelter, food and drink, so hotels it is then! As a consequence, his wife Laurel, never really knew *real* home life. After they left the mining city, she lived in the hotels her husband bought and sold.

For much of the 21st century, home ownership in Australia was considered an aspirational right. In a land of sweeping plains, space seemed limitless. Even so, to Laurel's regret, she didn't really have one of her very own until they retired fifty years later. So in 1945, Ray returned to Broken Hill looking for a bargain and very bravely bought a property in inhospitable landscape eighteen miles north of Broken Hill. It was the rather dilapidated Yanco Glen Hotel. The old historical building was a wood and iron construction, pretty basic but with a verandah and a dance hall attached to it. Was this really the home of her own the woman was longing for?

Ray was a great storyteller and often regaled the customers with tall tales about his past lives as a miner and publican, but he seemed oblivious to his wife's longing for a home of her own. Eventually, the isolation and hard conditions became too much and after some years at Yanco, Ray sold out as they had done very well out of it. The building is no longer there, and unfortunately the famous original hotel was burnt down some time ago. Another piece of Australian history lost!

Over the years, Ray and Laurel owned six pubs, scattered around the north and south coasts of New South Wales. When Ray turned sixty and decided it was time to retire and rest their weary bones, he sought space and privacy. They settled on Maraylya, about 30 miles out of Sydney. It was a five-acre block settlement, with historical ties to the early settlers and army barracks near Windsor. The area is now used for chicken and egg farming, and mushroom growing. It was a long trip from the city each time and quite isolating. So how did this happen and why was it a secret for so long?

Apparently, the Maraylya land was purchased for $25,000, mainly with the proceeds of successful investment recommendations their son Jeff made to Ray in 1976 when he was working as a geologist for an exploration company. In a chance encounter with a prospector, some secret information was exchanged. On this tip-off, Jeff drove 80 miles to the closest phone box at McKinley to call his father and ask him to place orders to buy shares for himself and six others at their exploration camp. The investments were in Pancontinental Mining and others that had exploration licences in Northwest Queensland. The contract notes later revealed Ray bought at the lowest entry price, so he did well. Land purchased, they had their lovely new house built. For whatever reason, the contracts were mysteriously signed by the son, not the father for whatever reason, but it may have had something to do Ray's interesting relationships with the tax man at the time.

At last Laurel had a home of her own! What fun she had setting it up: growing roses, cooking in her new kitchen and playing at being a housewife in her very own home. Tragically, the dream didn't last long, as she was struck down with an incurable illness and the house was sold to cover debts. But this is not the end of the mystery. Further to this story, there is an even more bizarre connection … The lead prospector for the exploration company was a man named Ken Brown, a giant of a man, even for the big men of Northwest Queensland.

When son Jeff visited the mother in the nursing home not long before she died, he noticed a rather tall, big-boned, brown-haired nurse and enquired as to her identity, being somewhat intrigued by her resemblance to our prospector Mr Ken Brown of Mount Isa. She replied her name was Brown she was from Mount Isa, and as to Ken, he was her older brother. So, Jeff then told Laurel the story of how this nurse's brother was instrumental in what had happened regarding Maraylya and how she was with friends.

Nurse Brown was there when she passed away. Shortly after, at Laurel's memorial, Jeff, dressed in mourning black, sat alone. A recording of his mother's favourite song,

Danny Boy, was drifting through his consciousness. Sung by a choir, the arrangement was just as she used to sing it. On the way out of the chapel he passed people who loved his mother, many whom he didn't know, but whose lives she had touched in some way. "Enjoy your lovely home in the sky, Mum," he whispered.

The

Shoe Box

It was time for a clean-up of my overstuffed wardrobe. For 80 years, a wardrobe that I had taken pride in filling a wardrobe with beautiful clothes, shoes and bags, trappings that defined who I was and who I endeavoured to be over each life stage. But who am I today?

Am I the same young woman who slithered into the black brocade size 8 cheongsam from Hong Kong in 1964? Or the turquoise silk suit and matching hat I had made for my daughter's wedding 30 years ago in Sydney? Or those teetering white and green high heels I used to seduce my lover in London only 40 years ago? Should I keep the elegant and newer suit I first wore to conduct the choir or the one I wore at my preselection for parliament?

They say a cat has nine lives; well, it seems I have had nine also, my wardrobe telling the stories of my life, wearing everything from rags to riches – glamorous gold to poverty grey and grief-stricken black. No matter.

After a clearing up of my mind by writing my memoirs, it is now time to clean up the rest of the trappings of a long and eventful life. Who will want all this? Where will it go? To whom should I leave my treasures – treasures to me but not to them, those who can't know the ups and downs of a life both privately and publicly lived.

So, I choose, tears streaming down my face as I tenderly pick up the tattered silver sandals worn at my first wedding fifty-six years ago and slip them into the trash bag. Then, with a smile on my face, I carefully re-wrap the newer gold sandals, a symbol of recent happiness. The past is the past, and the future is here now, so the local charity shops get the best, and the tip gets the rest. When I leave this house, it will not be to another, but to a haven in the sky, wearing angelic white diaphanous chiffon and smiling at the shoppers in Vinnies snapping up my treasures of yesteryear!

Ebb and Flo

Ebenezer and Florence (known to their friends as Ebb and Flo) were an elderly married couple. They were happy most of the time, but as with all partnerships, their temperaments ebbed and flowed along with the tides of their seaside village. As was their custom, they shopped once a week on a Monday, because they thought that was the quietest day. As was also customary, they sometimes argued about what to buy at the supermarket. "Lamb chops with peas and mint sauce tonight," decided Ebb.

"And peaches and cream," muttered Flo as they meandered around the aisles, arguing about on what to drop into the basket.

Finally, one day, Flo had had enough of Ebb's sneaky ways and flounced off through the checkout without realising she had accidently put a can of peaches straight into her bag without paying for it.

Suddenly the officious store detective pounced on her as the alarm bells rang out and bundled her into the police car, surprising everyone, including herself. At the day of the trial, the courthouse was packed as she fronted the judge.

"What is the misdemeanour"? he thundered from the bench.

"Stealing a can of peaches, sir" gave the policeman.

"How many peaches in the tin?" he asked Flo.

"Six, Your Honour" came the reply.

"Then your punishment will be six days in gaol, one day for each peach. Have you anything else to say before I pass sentence?" he asked.

"Yes!" piped up Ebb, "she also stole a can of peas, Your Honour!"

One Month later …

Ebb is lonely. He only has his thoughts for company now that Flo's gone. No doubt she is having a lovely rest in gaol, after stealing that tin of peaches. Ebb sits and ponders … maybe he should not have argued with her in the supermarket and caused her arrest. After all, she is the cook and always knows what's on the menu!

He finds he has so much to do now. On top of all the making of his own meals, he notices how dusty the place gets when it never used to. Funny too that spiders know Flo has gone – they never used to drape their webs over the ceiling corners. These towels may be getting old too; they smell and hold the damp more than they used to. And where's Flo hidden the soap and the toilet rolls? And when will she be back? I wish I hadn't told the judge about our argument, that she also stole a tin of peas. I really don't mind peaches – and I miss her.

Hook, Line
and Sinker

Ladies, what is it that makes the world go around, that makes our hearts flutter, which joins us in that most universal of challenges? No, it's not avoiding tax, it's finding a mate!

I recently read a book called, *If I'm so wonderful, why am I still single?* offering strategies that will "change your life forever". Well, I found it much too serious, so today I'm going to give you one strategy that I've had the most success with. For the men readers, it's a little insight into what makes a woman tick.

As we know, a bachelor is "an eligible mass of obstinacy entirely surrounded by suspicion". So, we have to be devious. Now, you may think this advice is not too appropriate at first, but read carefully, for here is some first-hand experience that worked for me – go fishing! Yes, it was in Sydney that I caught my Shark, in Portugal my Prawn, and in Scotland my Salmon. Do I see disbelief your eyes? You think this is beginning to smell like a fishy tale? That I don't look like a fisherman?

Outward appearances can be deceptive – they say it's not the wrapping on the parcel that counts but what's inside it, but believe me, in this game the wrapping is *all* that matters! Oh, I'm sorry, you think I've thrown you a red herring when you're still waiting to hear about my shark? Here, I'm afraid girls, I must let the men into our secret, for my reference is not Izaak Walton's *The Compleat Angler,* but a yet unpublished volume called *Hints for the Female Angler on How to Net Her Catch.* For catching a man and catching a fish are basically the same. Men fish in the maelstrom of the marketplace hoping their investments will yield a handsome dividend, but women do their angling in a more subtle way, and with a tasty bait and colourful lure the men fall for – hook, line, and sinker!

First, choose your spot. This, of course, depends on the species of 'Pisces' you're after. Around the city pond is the powerful shark, a calculating heartless streak of gleaming gunmetal, ruthless in business and with women. You know the kind that in an effort to retain his power, answers the telephone whilst making love! To catch him requires a tough line with heavy breaking strain and plenty of tenacity. Here, also, may be found the goldfish and sardine, both too small, not worth the effort, so throw them back – there are plenty of bigger fish in the sea.

In the office pool, you may find a bloater to your taste, all puffed up with his own importance. A barbed hook will soon deflate him enough to lure him into your trap. He is not the most handsome of species but can usually be relied on to provide a tasty meal.

We can't all live on champagne and oysters, but if that's your heart's desire, put salmon on the menu. Rich pickings are to be found on the upper reach of the Hawkesbury and better parts of Whale Beach. The sleek thoroughbred swishes along in his shiny Rolls Royce as he fights his way upstream, flicking the minnows away with an elegant tail. This one requires more investment in tackle and bait, but the return if netted is worth it (hopefully in diamonds).

Now that we have chosen the spot and species, let's prepare for the expedition with a visit to the beauty parlour and, of course, the boutique. This is a lengthy procedure known to take hours or even days for it is vital to be decked out in the correct attire. It involves many heart-searching decisions on what to wear. Not for the female angler the muddy, black gum boots and tattered cap smelling of last week's rotting worms. The rules are to smell and look as alluring as possible – the hook suitably camouflaged, for all's fair in love and war!

So, there you are, face painted, hair primped and body perfumed ready to face the world in all your glory and to go fishing in your favourite spot. Then patiently, as the spider weaves the web, you cast your line and sit and wait for a bite. And you have one!

The next step is to examine your catch and if he has pleasing shape and legal size, waste no more time. Don't let him be the one that got away. Net him, for he has taken the bait hook, line, and sinker!

So, there you have it. I am always dressed in the right gear to go fishing. Why not try it yourself? It worked for me!

Temptation

A frisson of anticipation ran through Carmen's body, clutching at her heart. She knew she was in danger, taking a risk shopping on this street, but still she continued, powerless to stop once she had taken the trouble to park the car there. Grabbing her shopping bag and summoning her willpower she mentally renewed the vow she made to herself that morning, the vow to become a new person, to leave the old behind – she would go to the gym.

Yes, she knew she really should take a good hard look at her diet and her penchant for exotic sweet morsels of sin. So, walking quickly past tempting shop windows, admiring longingly the lovely clothes on the elegant slim mannequins in the windows, she quickened her step. Suddenly, her eyes caught sight of the most colourful tempting display of delicious-looking pastries and cakes, and she could not tear herself away.

There were trays of perfectly cut custard slices topped with the most luscious pink shiny icing, crisp almond croissants, soft succulent apple turnovers oozing gooey cream, and large square chocolate-coated lamingtons. What a smorgasbord! Her stomach rumbled, her eyes lit up and her mouth watered.

No, I will not give in to temptation like I did before, she thought, mentally choosing which one she would buy. And so, as she slid into that den of wicked indulgences near the gymnasium, she vowed she would start her diet tomorrow.

As Carmen waited at the counter, she remembered catching sight of herself in the bathroom mirror that morning. *Quelle horreur*! She didn't imagine she was as unfit and out of shape as her soft, pudgy tummy, not-quite-yet double chin, and flabby arms reflected back at her. *Hmm.* Obviously, walking was not enough exercise. Then came a bright idea. She would diet, walk more and even go back to the gym.

She knew she had commitments, responsibilities. But at her age she didn't need to be quite so strict with her diet, her looks and her time. She was now her own person, she could go anywhere, be anyone, eat anything, couldn't she? Couldn't she? But she was lonely and if she wanted a new man in her life, she would need to smarten herself up.

Reminiscing dreamily, she remembered the last time she exercised, her astonishment at the array of pecs, muscles, abbs, throbbing chests and panting heaving bodies. Tarzan on a running machine, tiny leopard print tights moulding his glutes. Batman on his bike, bright blue shirt billowing behind him. And Superman glowing in red, straining his bulging arms. Gleaming sweat skimming over his toned torso; legs and arms straining to hold the weights (face concentrating on not dropping them so as not to appear to be weak); showing off his beautiful body to all who wanted to watch. Her eyes strayed as her body pumped, the pain in her back growing worse with each surreptitious glance. What a selection!

She turned her face away, embarrassed at the thoughts running around in her head, then down through her body, her legs and other parts she had not thought of for a long time, much too long. Was she displaying signs of the deadly sins – pride, lust, greed, envy and gluttony? Was she a sinner or could she be saved? Did anyone see her puzzled but wishful face as she peddled furiously on her exercise bike? She always believed she was a strong-willed woman, single yes, but still a woman, not yet old, able to overcome adversities of all kinds – divorce, poverty, loneliness, overweight, temptation.

As a girl brought up in a Christian family where sex was not mentioned and 'that talk' about one's body and what it did was held in private, her sex education comprised these warning words instilled by her mother: "Don't ever let anyone touch you down there". This was the era where virtue was valued, and sex education had not yet squirmed its way into the classroom.

Then Carmen started to discover what boys were about. Her first encounter with that advice, as she remembered, was when she was home from boarding school for the holidays and 'tarted up', she sashayed off to the local Saturday night dance. As she was only 14, her father used to come and pick her up at eleven o'clock, except for one night when he couldn't. Imagine her delight when Barry, the handsomest boy in town, a very dishy 19-year-old, asked to drive her home in his own 1959 Holden ute!

It was a moonless night as he parked the 'passion wagon', as it was known in those days, under large shade trees. He cut the engine, one hand sliding carefully along the seat to her leg, gently turning her face to his. She froze, heat pulsing her body, legs trembling. Suffice to say that all he got in answer to his "Well, are you goin' to come across?" was a chaste kiss. What did that mean, she wondered, embarrassed not to know. Her heart beating madly, she fled home through the bush in the dark, wondering longingly what his real grown-up kiss would have been like and what "comin' across" really did entail!

It was the 1960s and the hit song on the milk-bar's jukebox was Paul Anka's *Diana*, The Beatles were enjoying their first hit, *I Wanna Hold Your Hand,* at parties they were dancing *The Twist*, and Carmen was playing the *Black and White Rag* by Winifred Atwell on the piano. She often made her own clothes and took great trouble ensuring the starched, white rope petticoats were stiff enough to hold out a full circle of the emerald-green cotton skirt she had made, as she swirled around the rock and roll dance floor. An off-the-shoulder pale blue silk blouse and white high heels or flatties completed the flirtatious ensemble.

But stop dreaming, she chided herself! That was long ago and now I live for the present. Her dreams were of finding another partner and taking up sport again, and to share life with a special someone. She knew that every journey begins with a single step, and as she thought about tentatively dipping her toe into the water, she knew she was going to love this new journey. A journey hopefully not to heartbreak, but to heartfelt love. She took a moment to remember the last time she felt that. It was quite a few years ago now, but the longing was still there. Just as magnets are drawn inexorably to each other, so they were too, the underlying magnetism of a fatal attraction, an attraction that was not only foolish but unknowingly illegal.

It was at a company function when Carmen became aware of this handsome man standing near her. so almost accidentally brushing her arm against his, she introduced herself. As they touched, a frisson of primeval lust throbbed through her body. She knew he felt it too, as his eyes locked onto hers, oblivious to the crowd around them, the magnetism pulling them together. He called himself Rick, and because he was a public figure, making it all the more exciting, their dates were furtive phone calls at work, faxes in coded text and secret meetings, making it all the more exciting.

Their first date was at a typical country pub, a not altogether romantic place to meet. She will never forget Rick's first romantic gesture though, the waiter dashing out the back and returning to present her with a huge bunch of red roses, just like in the movies! This was followed by a kiss through the car door on his departure that sent shivers down her spine and left a smile on her face!

Was it coincidence or fate that saw them 'accidentally' meeting at the running track the next day on her morning walk in her little white shorts and Rick in his sexy cycling gear? One look at those muscly legs and she was hooked! *Yes, getting older is not a sentence, it's an opportunity* she thought, *an opportunity to be brave.* Their affair was brief, intense, and ultimately hopeless. There were furtive nights away, weekends and country trips under assumed names. The excitement, the lust, the fun!

But as the phoenix flies too close to the sun and ultimately burns up, so to their passionate affair became too hot to survive and her dream came crashing down. It was almost midnight, and Carmen was asleep in her lonely bed, when she was jolted awake by the shrill ring of the telephone. A woman's voice sobbing on the phone gave her such a start.

"You don't know me; I am his wife.

Carmen froze, her whole body in shock.

"Please, please Carmen, I'm begging you to let him go. Yes, I know we have been living apart and he is besotted with you, but his family needs him now!"

Her heart thudded, her pulse sped up to a crescendo that sent black specs whirling across her eyes followed by a sick feeling in her stomach she recognised as guilt. With a shock she realised who this was, the person you would be when you found a hole inside you, when someone had dug out your heart. She didn't answer, feeling too fragile. Her knees gave way, she sunk to the floor, time passed. Slowly and carefully, she hung up the phone and started to cry.

Carmen knew what had to be done. She had to let him go. How could she inflict this much hurt, how could she continue with this deception? She got to her feet and staggered back to her cold, empty bed. Try as she might she could not erase that phone call from her mind. She knew that by herself and her lover resisting temptation they were doing the right thing. As with any drug, then began the slow painful process of withdrawing from the deadly desire of addiction. Carmen knew Rick still loved her but sadly she never saw him again.

As she came back to her senses, she thought how times have changed in how to go about meeting a mate. People now use weird mobile phone apps like Twitter and Tinder. Swipe right? Yes! Swipe left? No! Whatever happened to the slow burn of romance, that sudden frisson of electricity? Can she ever feel that first-time kiss again? Temptation, temptation …

maybe I don't need a man in my life she thought … oh darn it, starving for beauty is just too much trouble.

"I'll have the chocolate cake, please" she whispered to the salesgirl.

The

Little

Red Car

It sat there smugly, beamig, red, bright red, taunting me with its cheeky grin. It smiled at me every time I passed its pristine gleaming glass prison confining its beauty to all but the observant. I passed it every day as I swooped by on the bus past its home, up the auto mile of Parramatta Road. It shone so red it glowed, its siren call wooing me until the day I finally succumbed. After all, I needed wheels, didn't I? A perky little design, I thought, just what I needed after a traumatic few years and returning to my homeland penniless, carless, and lonely after living overseas. That glamorous showroom on the Champs Elysees of Sydney beckoned me in, tempting me, helpless to resist. Wondering how I could afford it, the price tag way out of my reach, I dreamed it was mine. I pictured myself zipping around town, hair flying in the wind, kids in the back screaming with delight.

Yes, transport was not a luxury, it was a necessity. I had children to ferry to and from school, shops to plunder, people to see. *I needed it!* Then one day, joy of joys, lady luck finally smiled at me! I got a job with a real salary and didn't need to fight my desire any longer. Forgive me, but I succumbed to its siren call. "Pick me," it whispered, as I wandered starry-eyed among the exhibits. You couldn't miss it anyway, it was so bright with its headlight eyes sparkling, its silver bumper bars gleaming, and cheeky, ruby red duco beaming. I loved it! So, with some haggling my father would be proud of – Who wants to be seen in last year's model? I asked the salesman, "You won't be able to sell it, it's out of date already! I valiantly tried to lower his price tag, and then at last, amid much giggling, batting of eyelashes and fanfare, the deal was sealed. Ruby was mine!

What adventures we had, that cheeky little red car and me. They began with quite a bang. It was the school holidays, 1987, and my sister Roslyn and her little boy, and myself and my two young school aged children had been invited to my uncle's place at Coffs Harbour up the coast. Two single mums relishing a free holiday. Car boot piled high with bags, food, beach gear, and toys we excitedly set off.

Ruby was a hatchback model, but she thought she was a roadster. Along the motorway she sped my new shiny red car, valiantly trying to keep up with the big boys, little new heart beating wildly with excitement. It was a very tiring bumper-to-bumper trip northwards (did I mention it was Boxing Day?). The temperature was sitting on 40 degrees outside and about 50 inside, the air conditioning not coping with so many hot sweaty bodies. There was no fast M1 motorway in those days, just a two-lane highway chock-full of holiday traffic. Finally, there came a break, and at last we were free, zipping along through the next town.

Oops! I suddenly remembered that Taree had a reputation for officious policemen bent on catching speeding demons. *Phew*, I thought as we cleared the town, put my foot down and took off with glee. Many rude kid jokes and games of I Spy out the window later, it wasn't long before we heard the dreaded "EE-aw, EE-aw" of the siren bursting through our euphoric singing of *Driving along on the highway, honey.*

Reluctantly pulling over to the side of the road, I wound down the window.

"Yes officer?" I asked sweetly, eyes wide open with guile.

"Licence please, madam," he barked.

Timidly I offered my driver's licence.

With a puzzled look, he asked, "Do you realise what the speed limit here is and what speed you were driving at?"

"No, officer," I replied meekly.

Then, with growing annoyance from him: "This is a UK licence!"

(Did I not tell you that I had not yet bothered to change my driver's licence to Australian from British?)

"I am so sorry, officer, I have only been back a few months, and I didn't know I had to get an Australian one so soon," I sobbed, pleading ignorance.

But the kids had had enough, yelling, pulling each other's hair, fighting with boredom in the back seat. "I feel sick", "I need to go to the toilet, Mum!" they cried.

Sensing defeat was imminent, the policeman sighed, "Oh, go on then, but change your licence as soon as you get home."

Grinning widely, we gingerly pulled out on to the road again and set off, putting as much distance between us and him as we could. However, the drama was not yet over for us. An hour later, sliding around a treacherous bend on the side of a mountain, suddenly we went skidding wildly on the gravel. *Whump-whump-whump.* Oh no! To add insult to injury, we now had a flat tyre. The kids were screaming in my ear, my sister pale with fear and Ruby's little heart was beating as wildly as mine as we came to a stop.

Out we all tumbled to unpack the trunk to release the spare tyre, luggage, and kids' stuff strewn higgledy-piggledy out on to the road. How embarrassing to subject my dear little Ruby to such a public indignity!

My willowy sister and I attempted to lift the tyre off and change it, but we had no chance. Then the familiar sound of a motorbike came screaming to a halt next to us.

"You, again. Are you still causing trouble"? the officer snarled.

"I seem to have a flat tyre, and I can't get the spare out of the car," I replied.

"Not your lucky day Diana, is it?"

I looked into his face and oh my goodness, it was the same officer who had pulled us up before! What a disaster! What to do now? Unperturbed, he looked us over and frowned. Obviously, we were too much trouble to be seen cluttering up his road on a holiday weekend. Sighing audibly, he picked up his radio and sent off an SOS to his bikie mates. Within five minutes and with much fanfare two more motorcycle cops screeched to a halt. They looked with horror at the carnage on the road and didn't know whether to laugh or cry when they saw what needed to be done. With much rolling of eyes, heaving and heavy breathing, they removed the dead tyre and affixed the new one, and even gallantly loaded our luggage back into the boot.

"Would you care to join us for drink at Coffs later to show our appreciation officer?" I asked sweetly.

Looking at my gorgeous blond sister with interest, but then at the kids with horror, he declined the invitation. My Sir Galahad tipped his hat and revved up. "Don't let me see you on my road again, Diana!" he shouted as they roared off into the distance.

Too many hours later, we limped into town. Lesson learnt and new license applied for that week. But still Ruby's adventures continued. As a self-employed consultant, advising and training staff in local government, I followed the road wherever it led me, travelling wherever I could to convince the client they needed me, often staying at small motels for country assignments, on a limited expense account.

Navigating and sometimes driving along unknown dirt roads, I once nearly careered off a mountain track optimistically tagged a 'highway' on the way to the Snowy, over the pass from Tumut to the coast. The gravel was loose, and Ruby seemed to have a problem with keeping her balance. My heart in my mouth, she skidded wildly, me willing her not to succumb to the frightening drop below. We fought valiantly, steering in a panic to correct the slide. At the last minute she completed the turn, and we miraculously survived, facing the right way just as a timber truck pushed past us with an indignant swoosh and a very loud blast of his horn. However, the adventures of the little red car still had not finished! Back home some years later,

I was thinking Ruby was looking a bit worn and she may need to be pensioned off and retire to that bone yard in the sky. She was parked outside my flat in a not too salubrious area in the western suburbs.

Arriving home one night, I found to my horror that she was not her usual bright red self. She appeared to be weeping, as though she understood we were parting company. Her headlights drooped, her once shiny duco pitted and dulled, and there were wet tear-like streaks down her side. On inspection, I saw that ugly white stripes had been painted all over her – she had been the victim of a graffiti attack. My beautiful ruby red car had been brutally vandalised! The cause remains a mystery, but maybe the cheeky little lady was too much of a temptation in that not so salubrious part of Sydney, who knows? So, it was time to tearfully say goodbye to Ruby and find a shiny new car to take her place.

Yes, I still mourn the sad ending to my little red car, the fond memories, and the adventures I had with her … especially of Sir Galahad and his Knights of the Highway who taught me the value of humility and to always have your lipstick on and a good excuse ready for any occasion!

The

Orange Cat

In 1803, there took place one of the greatest and most adventurous navigational exploits the world had ever seen. Who went, and why? Was it because of greed, the search for riches, for new land, new experiences, and new medicines? Or was it the invention of the telescope, the magnetic compass, and lighter cannons for shipboard warfare? No, it was the colour orange!

Orange is the colour of sunshine and of warmth, and the colour of a delicious, useful, juicy fruit. Oranges contain vitamin C and prove to be what, along with cabbages, (that Captain James Cook discovered) stopped long voyage ships' crews from getting that dreaded disease scurvy (as Captain James Cook discovered)!

And so, in 1793, one of our great heroes of Australian history, Matthew Flinders, together with a motley crew, embarked on a series of round-the-world adventures to discover "The Great South Land". He did not however, travel alone. He had a companion. He took Trim, his beloved cat!

Trim was the most impertinent character, fearless yet affectionate, and he soon became one of the seagoing families. As the ships explored the unknown southern world over many years, he became the most widely travelled cat in history! Trim lived his own life and faced many challenges, made his own future, and eventually his own end.

Trim's story can teach us to discover how we can also be wise, fearless, happy, smart, and loved but above all, resilient. Oh, and one more thing, Trim loved oranges!

Trim's story was written by Matthew Finders himself and published in 1803.

***

This little story was inspired by my grandson's feline friend.

The

Postcard

It was at the local market as I was scrounging about for hidden treasures that I spied it on the table of discarded books (to me, a table of mystery!). Scrambling about, I chose a cookery book that seemed to be about times in the 1940s. To my surprise as I was leafing through it something fell out. It was an old, coloured postcard, now sepia grey and faded grey with age and from its duty keeping places as a bookmark. I couldn't wait to get home and start reading.

The picture dating from around 1930 was of an interesting looking country hotel. Was it a memento maybe bought when someone was on holiday that, still treasured, had been kept for the next person to find? Or was it more important than that, being kept hidden away for so long?

The hotel was situated on what looked like a muddy road. The front view showed a two-storied timber frame building with a slatted verandah that looked as if it would have been painted in dark green, white and black.

The front facing the street with façade had beautiful, printed posters attached to the wall that encouraged everyone to come and have a beer. It also promised accommodation with bedrooms and bathrooms, outside toilets, a lounge room and a balcony where guests could take their leisure.

The foreground showed a centre nature strip planted with Morton Bay fig saplings that divided the two roads, with rough, muddy footpaths on either side, inviting a future with shops yet to be built.

Peering deep into the photo, I felt a frisson of excitement run down my spine. Was it my imagination or could I faintly hear a Chopin waltz being played on a piano tinkling from the balcony? But I digress. Picking up the postcard and quivering with excitement I turned my attention to the elegant pen and ink handwritten note on the back.

Built by my grandfather Francis Tyson around 1930. (He transferred the licence from his Fernmount Hotel near Bellingen). There were only 2 or 3 houses nearby at the time. What great foresight he had!
Regards, Joyce Edwards.

What a mystery! Who was he, who was she and what became of Mr Francis Tyson and his granddaughter? I wondered if I could find out! With a little research I discovered that it was at that time that the Kumbageri Aboriginal people hunted and fished in the creek they knew as Bongol Bongol. But in 1861 new settlers arrived to disturb their peace and a small community emerged. The fledgling colony was growing and civilisation encroaching, bringing with it families, risk-takers and scoundrels. With all the growth, entrepreneurs dealing in building and furniture materials were in short supply.

One such foresighted settler was a Mr Walter Harvey who arrived with a bullock team to retrieve cedar logs that had been washed ashore on the beach. That helped him with setting up a nice little business. A Mr Oswald Sawtell then decided to stay for the cedar, and a small village emerged.

The population at that time was about 150. In summer, the village was swelled by campers and tourists attracted by the warm, north coast summer bringing holiday makers. But the tiny settlement still lacked a 'town heart', with the result that accommodation was not adequate for the sudden influx, and a lack of governance meant that littering and lawlessness was rampant. So, in order to progress, the town council voted to investigate to find a solution and appointed Sergeant Johnson to oversee the project.

After excited and sometimes heated discussion by the locals, a hotel was proposed. I could imagine that this happened only after much scratching of heads and arguments for and against were raged by the drinkers and non-drinkers. Why was this needed, they asked, as Sawtell was only 19 miles from Bellingen and close to Bonville and not too far from Fernmount where the population was larger? But there were few places to stay.

Here was an ideal opportunity to make his mark, thought Oswald Sawtell! With a post office that opened in 1927 a public school in 1928, the town was ready for something more adventurous, and a pub would provide a meeting place and accommodation. *So, it was not even new*, I thought with surprise, but built by Francis Tyson who transferred the license from his Fernmount hotel near Bellingen. There was great excitement when the first mention of the matter of a new town settlement on the north coast came to the public's attention, and lengthy and protracted proceedings for this most momentous occasion of a new hotel began. At the local assizes at Bellingen, evidence was given to the Licensing Inspector by Sergeant Johnson as to its necessity.

The Inspector, carefully grasping his lapel, replied that "to remove the license from Fernmount to a new building at Sawtell, it would need to be built of fibrocement and brick instead of wood because of the weight and fire hazard".

Subsequently at the Court in Coffs Harbour a license fee of fifteen pounds was applied for.

"A license is definitely necessary as strong drink is too readily handed out to young people underage and needs to be kept under better control of lawlessness" argued Sergeant Johnson.

What foresight! I thought, as there were only a few houses back then, as well as an early railway, a baker, butcher and general store. The only accommodation was a boarding house and, sadly, nowhere for the residents and visitors to meet and legally drink.

Cow dung and horse droppings mixed with mud often covered the area that seemed to be the natural roadway, the sea air wafting sweetly over everything, trying, unsuccessfully, to cover the smell of people, sewage, garbage and animals.

At last, the day had come when plans could be submitted. People dressed up in their Sunday best, the Coffs Harbour newspaper attended court every day, and the Inspector intimated that he would approve the matter if suitable plans were submitted including street work and the removal and replacement of the stinking sewer down the main street and replaced with proper drainage and street layout. The engineer added that his men were not going to work for 'starvation wages'.

The Women's Temperance Society argued that "drinking of liquor should not be permitted on the footpath where righteous and god-fearing citizens can walk safely".

There were plans for a butcher, why, there was a bakery with 100 loaves being baked every day, but no provision for sewage systems, electric light or other comforts!' After much toing and froing, it was judged – with just 116 votes and much cheering by the men and clucking of tongues by the ladies – that a Public House could at last be built for the convenience of the public. And so they planned for the hotel's installation. The actual relocation was an amazing feat involving the removal and transport of parts of the old hotel from its current site by trucks and horse and cart, much of it over rough bullock tracks through bush.

The journey began smoothly – a fine day to start such an adventurous project, Oswald thought – but the mountains were notoriously treacherous. It began on the horizon, a dark spot growing larger with every puff of wind, like a flock of crows flying closer. As dusk fell on the first day, a sudden bolt of lightning flared, sheets of icy rain battered branches and slashed at their backs, horses struggled through the mud, uphill and down dale, seeking shelter where there was none, a terrifying prospect and all for a dream. The party barely slept, tiredness and a dry ache in their eyes dulling their senses. Wrapped in oilskins, they struggled up and down slippery tracks over the rugged mountain miles through the national park and up to the coast to finally reach their destination, arriving to a hero's welcome.

Slowly, the land was sub-divided, and the railway arrived in 1925. At last, the day had come, and the town came of age with a post office, a primary school, a grocer, a dentist, a chemist and even a butcher shop with a refrigerating plant. Next came a meeting hall complete with dance floor, with entry at one shilling per head. The dance hall revenue in 1931 was 122 pounds and there was even talk of a moving picture theatre!

The fifteen pound hotel license was finally granted in 1932. I imagined the day of the opening, the newly refurbished hotel and the whole town dressed in their finery coming out to rejoice. The clatter of horse-drawn drays, wooden barrels of beer being off-loaded at the hotel and rolled down the cellar by brawny men, crates of bottles of spirits, and shouts of joy as a beer keg was tapped open and a fun evening followed.

Of course, a favourite hobby of young boys was collecting empty lemonade, beer, whisky and rum bottles for pocket money. Meanwhile, the young girls would have skipped around giggling at the ladies in fine dresses, the gentlemen in hats and coats, and the mayor resplendent in his suit and tie. The littler children would have been dodging around each other in excitement. The ladies would have celebrated at home as they did not drink in public but celebrated at home and it would be many years until they could. Looking at the postcard now, it's not hard to picture the scene of 100 years ago and, reading this, I realised I actually belonged in this years-ago-picture too!

The picture theatre lights still twinkle as they have done for many years, and as I peered deeply into the age-darkened photo I was suddenly taken back to an earlier memory. As a teenager myself I used to live in this pub in Sawtell! I could not believe the coincidence. It was a very different life from 100 years ago. My carefree summers and the backyard barbeque are what my teenage memories were made of; and Sawtell was a paradise for teenagers who loved surf, sand, sun, dancing and tennis. While living in Sawtell, the hit song on the bar's jukebox was Paul Anka's, *Diana*, and as I helped around the pub in the holidays the guys would serenade me! The Beatles were enjoying their first hit, *I Wanna Hold Your Hand*, and at parties we were dancing *The Twist*. And yes, I was playing Chopin on my piano on the balcony.

Today, the Moreton Bay fig trees stand majestic, huge, graceful branches spreading wide, illuminated in the evenings and a real feature like ethereal ghosts of times past standing guard over the town's 100-year-old history. But who knew that the town owed its prosperity to an adventurous and brave pioneer, Mr Francis Tyson? Thanks to his granddaughter, I do!

Strawberry

Ice Cream

❝Is this seat taken?"I looked up, surprised that on a crowded, early morning weekday train in Sydney people , where no-one talks to anyone else, where busy commuters usually don't have the manners to consider other commuters with their head in a book or newspaper, someone was talking to me. Not lifting my eyes from my book, I nodded "okay" and removed my handbag from the spare seat.

He sunk into it thankfully, relieved that he would not be standing the whole way into the city, and then turned to me apologetically. "I just had to tell you that you look like a strawberry ice-cream, in your little pink suit and white high heels."

What? Startled, I spun around to look at him. his eyes were saying *and good enough to eat*. Was an answer required? Does one say thank you for a compliment at the crack of dawn on public transport where proximity is almost inevitable, where one is more likely to pick up a disease than a compliment?

Our talk turned to everyday matters – weather, politics and the price of property. Oblivious of the other commuters, we sat looking at each other for a long time. Then suddenly the train jerked to a stop.

"Perhaps we will meet again," he whispered as he made for the doorway and alighted onto the platform.

My heart skipped a beat. Smoothing my sweaty hands over my rather short skirt, I silently thanked my girlfriend for donating such a sexy outfit to me when I had just arrived back home in Sydney, unemployed and lonely after living many years abroad.

It was the nineties and jobs were scarce. I was so out of work that that hand-me-down strawberry pink suit was really appreciated, and maybe even lucky I thought. Should I take this encounter on a train as a portent for the future, a torch light guiding me through my gloomy start in a new city filled with possibilities? Maybe I should even wear the same suit tomorrow? Should I take a risk? Look out for him or even follow him, or would that be creepy? Should I alight at the same stop as him, engage him in conversation, be friendly, charming, and flirty even?

In the end, I simply decide to place my briefcase on the seat next to me and to invite him to sit next time we meet. If there is a next time! We talk, finding common ground, commenting on the scenery and current affairs. Shyly, I take a peek at his profile and decide that he is an attractive man, not necessarily handsome, but certainly likeable. I notice he seems to like my company and fills me in on what's new with these parts of Sydney as we pass through each suburb that has grown and changed so much. I tell him about my new job in the city and how hard it was to find employment for someone over forty years of age. All too soon he stands to alight at Central Station. He picks up his briefcase and turns to me with a smile.

"Maybe we will meet again," he says.

Each day I watch the other travellers, faces flushed with early morning effort, shuffling along the platforms, pushing and rushing to board the train, hoping to find a seat to take a rest before the day's frenetic work pace. I note with surprise that since I have lived abroad, the colour of our population has changed and an interesting assortment of workers from other nationalities now piques my interest, like the shade of their skins, strange languages and dress. I watch students, smart in their private school uniforms, balance with the swaying train and clutch heavy-looking school bags; businessmen in grey suits and expensive looking ties; and smart secretaries decked out in tight skirts and mascaraed eyes, teetering on high heels hoping for a spare seat at every stop. There is Mrs St Ives, dressed in a sensible tweed skirt and a blouse paired with sensible black shoes. I guess she must be some sort of supervisor working in a large company. Other commuters glance my way at my wearing pink to work with looks that say, how frivolous! And also, no keeping seats!

The noise of the clackety-clack of the trains tracks on the rails, whooshing past each station, trees and houses a blur, the screeching to a halt as the next platform comes into view, seeking, seeking, are all new to me. I spend my time engaged in the scenery, the route from my station in North Sydney to the city, noting new houses amid tall featureless blocks that tower over the older, more elegant homes of yesteryear. What little greenery and playing fields are left are now surrounded by high-rise apartments that block the sun. I think how people and places change, but how we all have to accept that and look to the future.

Roads take the place of the lovely old homes built by early well-to-do settlers when quality mattered. Multistorey concrete and glass boxes dominate. Red tiled roofs and little corner shops where the grocer knew everyone seem to have gone forever. Residents are holed up in their private, hard-edged little flats.

My thoughts turn to my secret strawberry man, and I wonder if he will ever jump on my train again. Was our surprising connection all a fantasy? I call him Mr Gordon as that is where he first got on my train. Keeping my eye out at his stop each day, I sadly realised at the end of the week, he wasn't among those boarding.

At last it was Friday, and as the working week drew to a close I had given up ever seeing Mr Gordon again when suddenly, just as the train was pulling out from the platform, there he was running to board, a broad smile lighting his face as he spied me at the window. Jumping aboard and carefully weaving between other commuters, swaying as the train trundled along gaining speed, I noticed his briefcase carefully tucked under his arm and the other arm holding a box which he was shielding and protecting from bumps. Balancing the box precariously as the train swayed gaining speed, I could see he was looking out for me. I moved my bag as he sank into the seat gratefully.

As he settled down, I caught his sidelong glance and was rewarded with a shy smile as he nudged me to look into the box. As I carefully unwrapped it, looking around I was met with a broad grin, much to the delight of the curious commuters. My heart melted as I thought of the ways we could share those strawberries enjoying them together!

The harbour sparkled as we flashed over the bridge, glass multistorey towers now filling with busy bees. Pulling into the station, the sound and the unique smell of Sydney hit me. I was home and looking forward to my new life as a working woman. As we alighted, I waved to my travelling companion, my potential lover, my strawberry man. And yes, I was wearing the pink suit!

Singing

the Dream

Have you ever wondered just how dreams become reality? Well, let me tell you about how *my* dream of a non-auditioned Community Choir, the SeaSide Singers, became a reality in Nelson Bay.

My new husband Ron and I were attending church for the Christmas service in 2008 and the Tudor Singers from Newcastle enthralled the congregation with their rendition of Handel's *Hallelujah Chorus*. Of course, the audience was joining in too, with Ron and me singing our hearts out. I turned to Ron and said, "I like the way she conducts, and the joy such sounds can bring to people – I can do that!"

So how did we do it?

I put an advertisement in the local paper, and we subsequently welcomed over fifty prospects to the first meeting at our home in February 2009.

I had moved to Port Stephens in 2004, looking for a new life after retiring from paid work. I told them I was not a conductor but had graduated from the London College of Music and had numerous education qualifications. That seemed to impress, as when I asked if they would like to come along for the ride, all hands shot up.

Ron and I researched 'How to run a choir' on that wonderful reference book, Dr Google, and we were off! We chose the name to reflect our beautiful seaside area.

Sourcing sheet music was the next challenge, which saw us at auctions and second-hand bookstores in Sydney and Newcastle until we had enough to start singing in four parts: soprano, alto, tenor and bass.

Determined to sound and look professional, we also set about finding uniforms, and stage and sound equipment. To receive funding, we needed to be incorporated. Our new committee spent many hours each week setting up a constitution, protocols and procedures.

We practised on Tuesday evenings, firstly at our home, then at the Uniting Church until that became unavailable. We then moved to the Community Centre at Salamander Way. The singers willingly turned up each week and learnt their songs to ensure the show went on.

After only ten months, we had our first concert at the Changeover Dinner for the Rotary Club of Nelson Bay. Would our dream continue? Much was still to be done, and times were a-changing …

When the first piano accompanist left, I would play each part on the piano while Ron laboriously recorded them and then put them on a compact disc. Jenny (the computer whiz and choir librarian) would then compile CDs for everyone and print out the sheet music so they could learn the songs at home and at choir practices each week. After about five years in, we progressed to the Finale computer program and Samsung tablets, downloading the accompaniments. How the technical world moves on, even in the arts!

Of course, voluntary organisations don't run themselves, so with hard won sponsorship and seven willing helpers elected to sustain the choir's vitality, financial management and protocols and procedures, the choir recently celebrated fifteen successful years of making beautiful music together.

We have consistently had more than forty members, some who have rediscovered their love of music and singing after many years and now enjoy friendship and fulfilment through an educational and magical hobby that gives enjoyment through socialising and relating to the community.

Every year, we present a free concert for the senior citizen. One year, a local composer wrote a wonderful song called *Waltzing* about meeting his wife (who was now extremely ill) at a ball. I arranged it for three parts and on the day, Ron and I dressed up in formal ball gown and suit and danced while the choir sang it to the composer and the large audience. He and his daughter were overcome and so were we! It was recorded on a DVD so we could play it to his bedridden wife at their home. We all had tears running down our faces as she smiled in remembrance. The wonderful healing power of music!

The SeaSide Singers instigated the first Choral Festival in Port Stephens and have since run three very successful events (every second spring), with choirs from all over the state joining with us to make harmony and, of course, bring tourism dollars to Nelson Bay. A first for Port Stephens was a special concert with the young stars of Sydney Opera. We also initiated music workshops conducted by eminent performers and composers and toured to Lake Macquarie and Singleton for their music festivals.

One of my biggest thrills and challenge as a musical director was to conduct an operetta, *I Remember* by invitation of the Tilligerry composer, Vic Marden. It was about the 100th anniversary of World War One. The proud choir stepped up and sang so beautifully, performing twelve songs with David Scrogie as accompanist. Our solos were supported by costumed actors from Newcastle University. We performed, along with the Newcastle Army Band, in front of a large audience.

Next stop, the world! So, in 2018, we went international when a select group of twenty choristers travelled to Japan as part of the Port Stephens Sister Cities delegation for some concerts and reciprocal cultural activities. What a thrill for Port Stephens to reciprocate hosting a Japanese delegation and choir for the arts festival.

The SeaSide Singers has performed at hundreds of functions, festivals and concerts over the past fifteen years and I am so thrilled that the choir has continued to grow in strength, musicality, popularity and esteem in the community, all thanks to the loyal members and capable committee. What a joy it has been to see individuals find their voice and bloom, discovering their talent. I am also gratified by the many strangers in the community who tell me how much they have enjoyed our concerts, and so I smiled with quiet satisfaction when the choir was nominated for the award of Volunteer Cultural Organisation in Port Stephens. Yes, life is what you make it, for yourself and others, so dare to dream! Remember: "You don't sing because you are happy, you are happy because you sing!"

About the author

Diana Souter was born in Broken Hill and attended SCEGS Tamworth. She attended St Catherine's Waverley, UNE Armidale NSW, London College of Music and Slough Management College UK and UTS Sydney. She holds qualifications in Primary School Teaching, Adult Education, Human Resources Management, and Music. She has lived in Sydney, Melbourne and London and now Nelson Bay, combining careers of business with family.

Diana was a candidate for the Federal Elections for the seat of Grayndler and in 1998 and was a delegate to the national women's Constitution Convention in Canberra. She has travelled widely visiting over 43 countries and has three adult children and three grandchildren.

On moving to Nelson Bay in 2004 (supposedly to retire) she met and married Ron Souter (a singer) and in 2009 they established the first Community Choir in Port Stephens – the SeaSide Singers.

As a writer, Diana has has had many short stories published in magazines including in the NSW Government Seniors stories of 2022. A copy of her recently published memoirs '*From the Hill to the Bay*' by Diana Bennett-Mills-Souter is in the South Australian Library of Genealogy.